SWAN SKY

by Tejima

Philomel Books
NEW YORK

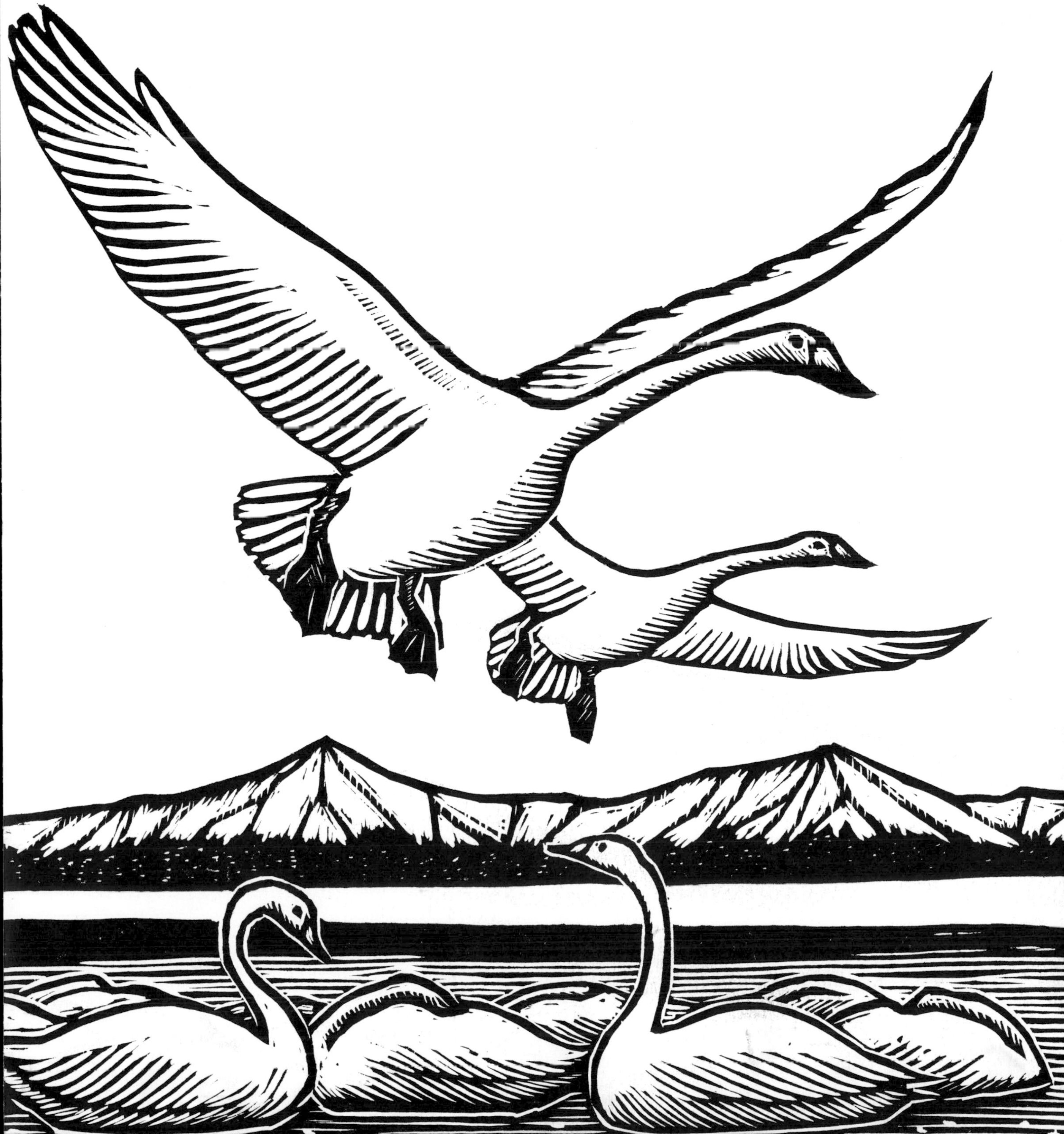

Far, far away there is a lake

where the swans go in the wintertime.

They stay there until the wind is laced with the first warmth of spring. Then, flapping their great wings, they honk a noisy goodbye. *Quoh, Quoh.*

They band together in giant Vs that stretch across the sky and start their long journey to their summer home in the north. For as long as they can remember, this is what they have done.

One year there is a swan who cannot go.

Her family stays with
her long after the other
swans have left. But no
matter how they coax
the little swan, she simply
tucks her head into her
soft, warm wings.

Spring comes to the cold land and flowers burst from the
earth and blossom.

Still the young swan does nothing but lie quietly
by the lake.

One night, after his family
has gone to sleep, the
father swan stands looking
at the moon. He realizes
the time has come when
the swan family will have
to return to the north
country.

The next morning, the other swans honk and honk. They want the little swan to come with them.

Her family flies in circles about her and fills the air with
sad cries.

But she calls back, telling them that she cannot go.

Finally, the swans dip their wings and fly north.

The young swan watches them fly away over the still, still water.

Soon the swans disappear beyond the mountains. The young swan's last goodbye echoes across the empty lake. She is alone.

Then suddenly, above the mountains the little swan sees white fluttering shapes. Her family has returned!

That night they rest together in the moonlight. The young
swan buries her head in her feathers.

As she sleeps, her family gathers around her. Before morning she dies.

At daybreak, saddened, the swan family flies toward the
north country.

When they reach their home, other
swan families have already arrived.
Nesting has begun. Still, the land feels
empty to them.

Then, in the cold sky, the morning light begins to break through the clouds.

The swan family thinks of the little swan.

And as the sun shines boldly down, they feel its gentle warmth. Spring has come again.

Quoh, Quoh, they call to the bright northern sky.

American edition published 1988 by Philomel Books. Text and illustrations copyright © 1983 Keizaburō Tejima. All rights reserved. Published in the United States by Philomel Books, a division of The Putnam & Grosset Group, 200 Madison Avenue, New York, NY 10016. Published simultaneously in Canada. Originally published by Fukutake Publishing Co. Ltd., Tokyo, Japan. Based on an English translation by Susan Matsui. Printed in Hong Kong by South China Printing Company. Designed by Martha Rago.

Library of Congress Cataloging-in-Publication Data Tejima, Keizaburō. Swan sky. Translation of: Ōhakuchō no sora. Summary: Despite the devoted attentions of her family, a young swan is unable to accompany them on the journey to their summer home. [1. Swans—Fiction. 2. Death—Fiction] I. Title. PZ7.T234Sw 1988 [E] 87-29228 ISBN 0-399-21547-6 First impression